The Adventures of
JELLY ELI Z.

Menucha Publishers, Inc.

Teacher Troubles for Jelly Eli Z.
ISBN 978-1-61465-361-5
© 2018 by David A. Adler
Typeset and designed by Deena Weinberg

A Pizza Contest for Jelly Eli Z.
ISBN 978-1-61465-362-2
© 2018 by David A. Adler
Typeset and designed by Deena Weinberg

A Baseball Problem for Jelly Eli Z.
ISBN 978-1-61465-647-0
© 2018 by David A. Adler
Typeset and designed by Deena Weinberg

Published and distributed by:
Menucha Classroom Solutions
An imprint of Menucha Publishers, Inc.
1235 38th Street
Brooklyn, NY 11218
Tel/Fax: 718-232-0856
www.menuchapublishers.com
sales@menuchapublishers.com

Illustrated by Dena Ackerman

Teacher Troubles for
JELLY ELI Z.

DAVID A. ADLER

MENUCHA CLASSROOM SOLUTIONS

CONTENTS

Chapter 1

NOT WiTH MR. MOSCOWiTZ

"ELI!"

"Huh."

"What's the answer?"

What's the answer? What was the question? What subject is this? Math? History? Science?

I look at the boys sitting nearby. A few are smiling. They seem glad Mr. Moscowitz caught me not paying attention. Benny's book is open and he's pointing to it.

"Book."

"Book! I asked you about George Washington's family, how many children he had. What kind of an answer is 'book'?"

I look at Benny again and see he's pointing to a picture in the book.

"Washington didn't have children of his own, but he had two stepchildren," Avi answers. "They were his wife Martha's children."

Benny still has his book open. I squint and look at the picture of Washington, his wife, and the two children. Washington's hair is white and puffy by his ears. It looks like a wig, but it's not. Men wore the wigs then, not women, but Washington didn't.

He powdered his hair to make it look white. You see, I don't pay attention in class, but I know things.

Avi isn't done.

"He married a widow named Martha Custis. She had a son and a daughter, Jacky and Patsy, so they became his stepchildren."

"Thank you, Avi."

Mr. Moscowitz looks right at me when he says that. Why would he look at me when he thanks Avi?

It's because he wants me to be more like him. That's why. He wants me to always listen in class, to always have the right answer. And I've tried. But how long can I listen to talk about the Revolutionary War? It ended more than two hundred years ago. Get over it, Mr. Moscowitz!

And long division, fractions, and decimals! Someone should make his math lessons into tiny tablets and sell them as sleeping pills. I don't know how Avi can keep his mind on that stuff. I don't know how Benny can. He's a good student, too.

"Why does he do that?" I ask Benny on our way home. "Why does he call on me when he knows I'm not listening?"

"It's his job."

"No, it's not. His job is to talk about history and number stuff. He does that. It's not his job to bother me."

"Actually, it is," Benny says while we wait at the corner near school. "He has to make sure we learn."

It's odd, I think. He gets paid to make me know that stuff. Why don't they just pay me? If they paid enough, I'd be happy to learn it.

Someone should rethink this whole school business.

The traffic light changes to green and we cross the street. Benny and I live on the same block. We walk together to and from school. He lives in a big house in the middle of the block with all his brothers and sisters. I think seven.

I live in an apartment in the corner building with my mother, grandmother, and sister. What about my father? Benny never asks me about him. Good friends are like that. They don't ask lots of questions.

Oh, and I have a nickname. People call me "Jelly Eli" because it rhymes and because I love jelly. Every day I go to school with a pocket-full of jelly beans. My favorite flavor is lime. I have jelly sandwiches for lunch, every day a different flavor. Today it was boysenberry.

I'm Jelly Eli Z.

The Z is the first letter in my last name,

Zipperbaum. That's some last name, isn't it? I once figured that in just one year of homework, and I get lots of it, it takes me many extra hours just to write my name. The next time we get one of those long writing assignments, the teacher should say, "Eli Z., you've spent so much extra time writing that last name of yours, you don't have to do the report."

I'm already in fourth grade and it hasn't happened. And I don't think it will happen this year, not with Mr. Moscowitz.

Chapter 2

THE BROWN-EYE EYEGLASSES

DID YOU EVER get that creepy feeling that you're being watched, that you're being stalked, that whatever you do, the same two eyes see it all? Well, it's actually four eyes. My stalker wears eyeglasses.

I got that creepy feeling today in school and I don't mean from Mr. Moscowitz. Right now my stalker is in the hall right by the door to our class and looking in. And don't tell me to report this to the principal, to Rabbi Goodman. He's the one watching.

This is the absolute worst day for this to happen. This is the day I finally figured out this school thing. You see, Mr. Moscowitz doesn't call on me to get answers. He's just trying to catch me when I'm not paying attention. So, if he thinks I'm listening, he'll be happy and won't call on me. And if he doesn't call on me, I'll be happy.

Do you understand? We'd both be happy. So here's what I did.

On our computer at home I printed pictures of two large brown eyes. That's because my eyes are brown. I made a pinhole in the middle of each of the paper eyes. Then I took the green glass out of an old pair of sunglasses and pasted in the eyes.

I put on the glasses and looked through the pinholes at the mirror by the front door of our apartment. It looked like someone with brown eyes was looking right back at me. My plan was to wear those eyeglasses in class. And since no one not wearing the glasses could look through the pinholes, no one would know what I was looking at, especially Mr. Moscowitz. He wouldn't even know if my eyes are open or closed.

This afternoon I put them on in class. I wore them for just a few minutes. Mr. Moscowitz even looked at me once. He looked a bit surprised, but that's probably because yesterday I didn't wear glasses.

But that can happen. I could have gone to the eye doctor after school and he could have told me I needed glasses and I needed them right away. There's a store near my house with a sign in the window that says, "Stylish Eyeglasses in One Hour!" Maybe I went there and got these stylish things. Maybe.

There I was, sitting in my seat, hiding behind two paper brown eyes, and I hear a noise by the door to our class. I look and there he is, Rabbi Goodman, staring at me through the window in the door.

I turn away and take off my brown-eye eyeglasses. I put them in my pants pocket and face Mr. Moscowitz. This time I really try to listen. This time there are two people watching me, Mr. Moscowitz and Rabbi Goodman.

Math.

He's talking about polygons.

That sounds like something someone would say when his parakeet flies off. "Polly gone!" But this is math and in math a polygon is a flat shape.

A triangle is a polygon.

Did you know that?

I wonder if triangles know that they're polygons.

Did you know that there are a lot of different kinds of triangles?

Isosceles. Obtuse. Equilateral. Scalene. Right. And then some triangles have relationships with others, like congruent triangles. They're exactly alike, like identical twins. And there are similar triangles. They're like two brothers, an older one and a younger one. They look the same, but one is bigger.

Now you're wondering why I'm telling

you all this. And I'm wondering why Mr. Moscowitz is telling it to me.

I guess that's what happens when I listen in class. I learn stuff. Now if I meet a triangle I can say to it, "I know you. You're George Isosceles. And I know your cousin, Jacob Scalene."

I look at the door. Rabbi Goodman is gone. Now only my teacher is watching me.

After math it's back to the Revolutionary War and nothing has changed. America still won.

I put my hand in my pants pocket. There's my pair of brown-eye eyeglasses. I'm tempted to put them on again. I'm tired of listening to all this George Washington stuff. But Mr. Moscowitz might think it's strange that I didn't wear them for the math lesson and put them on for history.

I take out a few jelly beans, two yellows

and an orange. Whenever Mr. Moscowitz turns away, I nibble on a bean.

I'll save the brown-eye eyeglasses for tomorrow.

Chapter 3

FLOWERS AND TREES

"FOURTEEN."

That's what I tell Benny as soon as we're outside of school. It's the answer to the question he no longer has to ask. "How many jelly beans did you eat during Mr. Moscowitz's class?"

Benny knows that the less I listen in class, the more beans I eat.

"That's not so many," he says. "I guess you liked learning about polygons."

"No, it's Rabbi Goodman. He was watching me. I must be in real trouble."

We are in the middle of lots of kids leaving school. Most of us live close enough to walk home. As we walk, boys go off in different directions until there are just the two of us, Benny and me.

"It's not you," Benny says. "It's Mr. Moscowitz. My dad knows him and this is his first year teaching and at the end of the year Rabbi Goodman has to decide if the school should keep him. He peeks in to see if we're all in our seats and listening."

We stop at the corner and wait for the traffic light to change.

"You mean, if I'm not paying attention he doesn't blame me, he blames Mr. Moscowitz?"

"He blames both of you."

The light changes to green.

As we cross the street I think, *This is one of those good news, bad news deals.* The good news is the principal doesn't think it's all my fault if I'm not listening to the lesson. The bad news is I could be the reason my teacher loses his job. Not good! It was Rabbi Goodman who once told us that we are all responsible one for the other. I don't want to be responsible for someone losing his job, even if he's my teacher.

My grandmother is waiting for me when I get home with a snack of jelly on crackers and a glass of milk. Every day it's a different jelly. It's my job to guess the flavor. I sit by the kitchen table.

"Close your eyes," she tells me.

That's because if I see the jelly is orange,

even before tasting it I would know it's orange marmalade. Red would be cherry, strawberry, or raspberry.

I close my eyes.

Grandma puts a cracker sandwich in my hand. I taste it.

"Caramel apple."

Grandma laughs and says, "You're right. Now tell me, how was school?"

"Okay."

My sister, Debbie, is on the floor coloring. She's four and she loves to color and not in coloring books. She colors on blank sheets of paper and on the unprinted borders of newspapers. Mom even cuts open empty cereal boxes so she can color on their insides. Her drawings are all over, taped to the walls of our apartment.

She's lucky. She doesn't get homework, but I do. I go to my room to do it. I'm working on a sheet with lots of polygons. I have to name them. I feel like naming them "Grover" and "Noah" and "Jacob." Instead I name the ten-sided one "Decagon," the five-sided one "Pentagon," and the four-sided one that looks like a squashed square "Rhombus."

There's a soft knock on my door.

"Come in."

It's Debbie.

"I made this for you," she says and gives me a paper covered with scribbles. "Do you know what it is?"

How could I know? I'm not even sure I'm holding it the right way. It might be upside-down.

"Yes, I know what it is," I tell Debbie. "It's a beautiful picture."

"It's flowers and trees."

She watches as I tape it to the wall near my desk.

Chapter 4

DOT, DOT, DOT

NOW THAT I KNOW Rabbi Goodman is checking on our class, I see him all the time. He walks by our door and stops, just for a minute, and looks in. And now that I know my teacher might lose his job because of me, I try very hard to look like an Avi. I don't mean the curly blond hair and neatly tucked-in shirt. I mean the paying attention part.

It's not easy listening to someone, anyone, talk about George Washington, triangles and quadrilaterals, and punctuation marks for minutes and hours and almost forever.

Have you ever heard of an ellipsis?

It's a punctuation mark. That's what Mr. Moscowitz talked about today. It looks like three dots because that's what it is. It means something is left out.

"Six."

That's what I tell Benny as soon as we're outside of school.

"That's all!"

"I paid attention. I know all about rhombuses and ellipses." I feel my pocket. "I still have lots of beans. Do you want some?"

"No, thank you," Benny answers. "They

always come with pocket lint."

I take two out, cherry and lime and some lint. Yummy.

We wait at the corner for the traffic light to change.

"So," Benny asks, "how do you like listening to an entire lesson?"

The light changes to green.

"I don't know how much longer I can do this," I answer as we cross the street. "A few times today I was about to sneak a jelly bean and I heard a slight noise. I looked through the door window and there was Rabbi Goodman. I think anytime he leaves his office to go somewhere he first goes past our room."

"He probably looks in lots of classrooms."

I shake my head.

"I've had the same seat all year, right by the door, and I didn't see him looking in until this week."

"It's close to the end of the school year. He must have to decide about all the new teachers."

My grandmother is waiting for me when I get home with a snack of jelly on crackers and a glass of milk. I sit by the kitchen table. I close my eyes and Grandma gives me the cracker sandwich.

"Orange marmalade."

Grandma laughs and says, "You're right."

I open my eyes and drink some milk.

"How was school?"

"Well," I say, "in math we learned all about quadrilaterals, you know, squares, rectangles, dot, dot, dot, and rhombuses."

"Dot, dot, dot," Grandma says. "What's 'dot, dot, dot'?"

"We also learned about that. It's an ellipsis. It means I left something out. I didn't tell you the names of all the quadrilaterals."

"Oh, that's fine. You don't have to tell me all that. You know, I have trouble with names."

"That why I ellipsised."

I like ellipses. I wonder if I could write my name "Eli Z...m." Do you see what I did? I ellipsesed my last name. I left out the ipperbau.

Here's my autobiography. That's what you call it when someone writes the story of his own life. Here's mine:

"I was born...and here I am."

Here are instructions on how to drive a bus:

"Sit on the seat in front, behind the big steering wheel...and now you know how to drive a bus."

Hey, I should use it in my homework.

Here's a report about George Washington:

"George Washington was born in 1732 and...he died in 1799." All the stuff about being a soldier and president is in the ellipsis.

Chapter 5

LiFE iS LiKE THAT

IT'S NOT EASY to sit in class all day and pay attention. That's what I told Mom and she said, "That's your job. Sometimes it's not easy for me to stand all day and fill prescriptions." Prescriptions are notes from doctors telling Mom what pills to put in those small plastic jars. "But that's my job and listening in class is your job."

Mom is a pharmacist. That means she works in a drugstore and she's not the woman behind the cash register. She's behind the drug counter. She prepares the medicines and she's nervous every time her boss comes into the store.

She gets paid for doing her job. I don't.

Right now I'm in the noisy, smelly school cafeteria.

"How can you eat that?" I ask Benny.

His lunch is always a cream cheese sandwich on whole wheat bread, unsalted pretzels, an apple, and a small plastic bottle of spring water.

"I like it."

"But it's the same every day, and cream cheese is so dry."

Benny takes a drink of water, wipes his lips with the napkin he takes from his lunch bag, and says, "That's why I bring water."

Jacob says, "I have lettuce, tomato, and yellow cheese on rye bread." He takes a bite and says, "Igh ghlood."

It's hard to understand what he says when his mouth is full of sandwich.

Jacob is not in our class but we always eat with him.

I say, "And I have jelly on bread. It's a different jelly every day and a different bread. Today it's raspberry on pumpernickel. It would be boring to always eat the same thing."

I take a bite of sandwich and then realize something. I tell Benny and Jacob, "That's why there are lots of jelly bean flavors. It would be too boring to have a whole bag of lime."

I take a handful of beans from my pocket

and put them on the table.

"You see, lemon, orange, cherry, lime, coconut, and black licorice."

"And lint," Benny says.

"Take some. I don't eat them all now that Rabbi Goodman keeps spying on our class."

Jacob takes a few. Benny doesn't.

I say, "Did you know there's a National Jelly Bean Day? It's April 22."

Benny is smart, but there are some things I know that he doesn't.

"Did you know it takes at least a week to make a jelly bean? Luckily, in candy factories they don't make just one at a time."

In class after lunch, I keep my eyes on Mr. Moscowitz and on the hall. Sometimes I'm looking right at Mr. Moscowitz but not listening to him. I'm thinking about a book I want to write, a jelly bean mystery. That's all I know about the book, but I know I want to write it.

I don't see Rabbi Goodman. Maybe he's not in school. Principals have lots of meetings. Or maybe he's already decided about Mr. Moscowitz so he doesn't have to check on our class.

The school day ends and I realize something. Mr. Moscowitz hasn't called on me the last few days. That's because he knows I'm listening in class. Only now, it would be okay if he calls on me.

Life is like that. Sometimes when you want something you don't get it, and when you get it you don't want it.

I open the door to our apartment and Debbie tells me, "You have to be quiet. I'm doing my homework."

She has no homework. She's not even in school. I'm the one who has homework and I don't want it.

It's like I said. Sometimes when you want something you don't get it, and when you get it you don't want it.

Chapter 6

THE BEiGE CLOTH BANDAGE

I'M AT LUNCH talking to Benny and Jacob. Plum on rye. That's my sandwich. Mr. Kogel comes to our table. He runs the lunchroom. He makes sure there are no fights and that we clean up.

"Eli Zipperbaum," he says. "Finish your sandwich and then go to the principal's office."

He walks away.

"What did I do?" I ask, but I'm not sure Benny and Jacob understood me. When I asked, my mouth was full of plum and rye.

Until this week I didn't pay much attention in class, but I never caused any trouble. I usually do my homework. I'm mostly a good kid. MOSTLY. Why does Rabbi Goodman want me?

Maybe he found out about the jelly beans. We're not allowed to eat in class.

Maybe he looked at some of my homework. Sometimes I don't put real answers to questions. I just make things up.

The lunchroom is in the back of the school. The office is right near the front door, so I walk past lots of classrooms.

Some kids don't have lunch now so they're in class. I look through the door windows and see lots of kids not listening.

Hey, I'm not the only one!

I walk into the office and Rabbi Goodman is sitting behind his desk.

"Zipperbaum," he says. "Your grand-mother is fine."

"I know that. I saw her this morning."

Rabbi Goodman tells me, "She fell and twisted her ankle. It's all wrapped. Your mother rushed her to the hospital, but now she has to get back to work. She wants you to go home and help take care of your grandmother and your sister."

"Are you telling me to go home?"

"Yes," he says and laughs.

Hey, I think. What's funny about a twisted ankle?

"Your mother said I have to tell you all

this," he says and then reads from a paper on his desk. "Don't run. Walk home. Walk on the sidewalk. Look both ways before you cross the street. Don't talk to strangers."

He smiles.

"You know all this and you live real close to school. Get your things and go home."

I leave his office, go to my classroom, and get my things. It feels odd leaving school in the middle of the day. Odd but good.

I wait at the corner and realize Benny is always with me when I wait here. We always walk together to and from school. But not today.

Mom is by the window watching for me when I get close to our building. I get inside and she opens the door for me.

"Debbie is playing in her room. Grandma is lying down. Don't let her do anything."

I put my books on the small table by the door. I left school before Mr. Moscowitz gave us homework, so I have the afternoon off.

"When it's time for dinner," Mom says, "Grandma will sit in the kitchen and tell you what to do. I'll try to get home early."

Mom works Sunday through Thursday. Tomorrow is Friday, so she'll be home.

Mom opens the front door and stops. She turns and tells me, "Thank you. I'm glad I have such a responsible son."

Me? I think as Mom leaves. I'm responsible? I guess I am.

Grandma and Debbie share a room. I look in. Grandma is on her bed. Her eyes are closed. I guess she's sleeping. Her right ankle is wrapped in a large, beige, cloth bandage. Debbie is sitting in the corner, on the floor, with papers and crayons. She's making more beautiful pictures.

It's much too early to prepare dinner. And anyway, without Grandma telling me what to do, I don't know what to cook.

I take a book and open it but I'm too distracted to read. I think about what I would be doing if I was in school.

Chapter 7

CHICKEN-FLAVORED JELLY BEANS

IT'S MONDAY AFTERNOON.

Grandma is getting around with a cane. She still needs help doing some things, but I'm able to go to school and Mom went to work. Right now I'm sitting in class trying to at least look like I'm paying attention to lots of talk about finding the areas of polygons.

I'm looking right at Mr. Moscowitz, so he thinks I'm listening, but I'm not. I'm thinking about my future.

One of Mom's friends asked her why she became a pharmacist. I was there. I heard her. And Mom said, "That's what I always wanted to be."

"Always?" I asked Mom. "What do you mean?"

"My brother, your Uncle Aaron, was sick. He was just three years old. We were very worried. It was the doctor who examined Aaron, but it was the pharmacist who gave us the pills that made Aaron better."

"If Uncle Aaron was three, you were six."

"Yes."

At six, Mom knew what she wanted to be. I'm nine years old. In the middle of the lesson on finding the areas of polygons, I decide I need to think about my future.

One thing is for sure. I don't want to be a teacher. If I was a teacher, I could get a whole class of students like me and I know I don't want that.

Mr. Moscowitz is not looking at me, so I reach into my pocket and take out two beans. Orange and lemon. I quickly put them in my mouth.

"Eli Z.," Mr. Moscowitz says, "how would you find the area of a rhombus?"

I quickly swallow the beans.

I think, *How would I find it? Is it lost? I'd probably try to remember where I last saw it and look for it there.*

I don't say that.

I think about squares. To find the area of a square, I would multiply the length of the base by the height. The area of a rhombus would be less because it's squished. The more it's squished, the less the space inside it, the less the area. The more it's squished, the less the height. So to find its area you would multiply the length of the base by the height just like with a square.

I say that.

Mr. Moscowitz is surprised. I got the right answer.

I told you before, I know some things. Actually, I didn't know this. I figured it out.

With the rhombus question Mr. Moscowitz had tried to catch me not paying attention, but I gave the right answer. Now he won't call on me for a while. That's good. I can eat beans and think about my future.

I could be a doctor. A surgeon. I'd cut someone open and look inside. "Hey, a chicken wing!" I'd take it out, show it to the patient, and tell him, "You should chew your food more before you swallow it."

Chicken wings! I'd rather think about jelly beans.

I could be a candy maker and make fancy flavors like fried chicken flavored beans. Every morning there would be hundreds of hungry people on line. Each would be waiting to buy three bags of Eli's Uniquely Flavored Beans. I'd make chicken flavored beans and French fry flavored beans and ketchup flavored beans.

"Eli! Eli!"

Benny is standing by my desk.

"Let's go. School is out."

This happens a lot. I start thinking about jelly beans and have no idea what's going on around me.

I gather my books and things. Benny and I are walking toward the door and Mr. Moscowitz says, "Eli, wait a minute. I want to talk to you."

Chapter 8

HERE iT COMES

WHAT DID I DO wrong?

I mostly paid attention. *Mostly* for me is good. I even answered a question. And I only ate six jelly beans.

Mr. Moscowitz stands by the door as the kids in my class walk past. Avi and a few of the others look at me as they leave. I'm

sure they want to know what I did wrong.

Benny and I wait by Mr. Moscowitz's desk.

All the other kids are out. Mr. Moscowitz turns toward us and looks right at Benny. He waits.

"Oh," Benny says. "You want to talk just Eli. This is private."

Benny tells me, "I'll wait for you outside."

We watch him leave the room.

Mr. Moscowitz sits at the edge of his desk. He smiles.

Why is he smiling?

"During lunch, I met with Rabbi Goodman. He spoke to me about my work. You know, this is my first year teaching."

Why is he telling me this?

"Do you know what he said?"

That's one of those rhetorical questions, the kind you don't answer.

"He said he's been looking in at my classroom. He wanted to see if my students were all in their seats, if they seemed interested in my lessons. Now this is why I wanted to talk to you."

Here it comes!

"He said, 'I especially watched Eli Zipperbaum. I like Eli. He's a good boy, but it's not easy to hold his attention. And you did. Even last Tuesday, the day he put on those strange eyeglasses, the ones with pictures of eyes pasted in. Even then, I think he was listening.'"

Mr. Moscowitz smiles and says, "He thinks I'm a good teacher because of you."

"He does?"

"Yes, he does. Thank you."

I'm not in trouble. I didn't do anything wrong. I did a whole lot of things right. I acted responsibly for my teacher just like

Rabbi Goodman said I should. I even acted responsibly for Grandma when she hurt her ankle. Not bad Eli Zipperbaum.

I start out of the room. I stop at the door. I turn and ask Mr. Moscowitz, "You knew about the eyeglasses?"

"Yes. I thought they were clever and you weren't bothering anyone."

"Oh."

Benny is waiting in the hall by the water fountain.

"What did he want?" he asks. "Are you in trouble?"

"No," I tell my best friend. "I'm not at all in trouble. I'm a bit of a hero. I'll tell you all about it on our way home."

And I do.

A Pizza Contest for

JELLY ELI Z.

Illustrated by Dena Ackerman

A Pizza Contest for JELLY ELI Z.

DAVID A. ADLER

MENUCHA CLASSROOM SOLUTIONS

CONTENTS

Chapter 1

IT'S NOT FAIR

PIZZA!

Rabbi Goodman is the principal of my school and he thinks *pizza* is a magic word. And if *pizza* doesn't do the trick, how about *pizza party*.

Listen to this.

Today, in the middle of math, he came

into our class. He didn't knock or anything. He just opened the door and walked in like he's the boss of everything.

Oh, yeah, he is.

"I have some exciting news," he said.

He paused, like he was too excited to tell us the news. So, of course, I got excited, too.

Maybe he's going to say we learned enough already so school will be closed for the rest of the week. And it's only Monday!

Maybe the water fountain in the hall is now a soda fountain. I hope it's an orange soda fountain.

Maybe there's a new rule that we can't get homework on any day that ends with the letter y.

Rabbi Goodman took a deep breath and told us, "The mayor announced the 'Take Care of Our Neighborhood' program."

Hey, that's not exciting!

"Our school will participate in a number of ways. First, we'll keep our classrooms clean. Second, we'll keep our play yard clean. And third, on our way to school and our way home, we'll pick up any litter we find."

Rabbi Goodman smiled.

"Here's the exciting part. This week, whichever class does the best job taking care of our neighborhood will have a pizza party next Monday."

That was this morning. Now school is out and my best friend, Benny, and I are walking home.

I tell him, "Everyone will be cleaning and cleaning and cleaning, and only one class will get cold pizza and warm soda. What about the rest of us?"

"Maybe our class will win."

Benny is an optimist. He's the kid who

buys a raffle ticket with a top prize of a trip to Florida, and as soon as he buys a ticket he begins to pack. He's sure he'll win.

I tell Benny, "Make sure you take along a baseball hat."

"What?"

"There are lots of great amusement parks in Florida and they're all outside. The sun shines all day even in winter and you don't want to get a sunburn."

"What are you talking about?"

The traffic light at the corner near school is red so we wait.

"I was talking about Florida."

"I'm not going there. I'm going home, and we were talking about the keep the neighborhood clean thing and pizza."

"Oh, that."

Lots of kids from our school are waiting at the corner. There's a crossing guard

who's usually there. He's an old man with a crossing guard sash and a badge who doesn't let us cross until the light is green and he's sure no cars are coming.

"Look!"

There's a candy wrapper across the street.

"I'm going to pick that up and throw it away and Rabbi Goodman won't even know, so how will he know which class did the most to clean the neighborhood?"

The traffic light changes to green. The guard looks both ways and waves to us, and we cross the street.

"I'm doing this," I tell Benny as I pick up the wrapper, "not to get cold pizza but because it's the right thing to do."

"That's good," Benny says, and he should know what's good. He's *always* good!

I put the candy wrapper in my back

pocket. I'll throw it out when I get home.

Benny asks me, "Would you be more excited if instead of pizza it was a jelly bean party?"

"Yes, that would be great. Pizza is just tomato sauce and cheese on crust, but jelly beans come in lots of great flavors. And with pizza you have to take a bunch of bites to eat one slice. With jelly beans you can eat a whole bean with just one bite. Watch!"

I take one from my pocket. It's lime, my favorite. I pop it in my mouth and chew. You have to chew to get the flavor.

I should ask Benny if he wants a bean because Rabbi Goodman has told us many times we must share our bounty with others. The first time he told us that, about sharing our bounty, I thought he meant our paper towels. You know, Bounty is a brand of paper towels. But he meant we should be generous and charitable. BUT, and it's an important but, I no longer offer beans to Benny because he always doesn't want any because he says they come with pocket lint.

I take the last two, orange and lemon.

Now here's something you should know. It's about justice and being fair and Rabbi Goodman has told us many times to be fair.

Here it is.

I'm Jelly Eli Z and the Z is for my last name, Zipperbaum. Lots of times I'm too busy to write it all so on homework papers I just write Eli Z. But I can't do that on state tests, you know, the ones where you have to use a number two pencil and shade in lots of tiny circles. I have to shade in ten circles for Zipperbaum. By the time I get to the Baum part other kids are already answering questions. They get a head start on me.

That's not justice. It's not fair and that explains why sometimes other kids get a better score on the state tests than I do.

Chapter 2

i KNOW JELLY

WE'RE STILL WALKING and I'm still looking for litter. You already know I'm not trying to win the pizza. I'm looking because, now say it with me: *it's the right thing to do.*

I ask, "Do you want to go to Florida?"

"Maybe."

"My grandmother says when she gets

old she wants to go there, especially in the winter because here it's snowy and cold and there it's sunny and warm. Whenever she says that I think, *When you get old! Grandma, you are old.* But I don't say it."

We stop again before we cross a small street. There's no traffic light, but we still look for cars before we cross.

We walk a bit without talking and then we both see the same thing. Next to a large red brick apartment building, in the bushes right by a corner window, are a bunch of papers.

Benny says, "Let's take care of our neighborhood," and we do.

We walk across the grass. There's a small crumpled white bakery bag and wrappers from two chocolate bars. We reach into the bushes and get them. Taking those things makes a rustling noise. Just as I'm pulling the bakery bag out, I hear another noise. It's from behind the window. I look up, but all I see is glass and curtain.

"Was someone watching us?" I ask when we're on the sidewalk again. "I think someone wanted to know who was next to the window. I heard something and looked up, but I didn't see anyone."

Benny is holding the two candy wrappers and the bag.

"I can take those," I say. "I still have room in my pocket."

I put the wrappers in, but not the bakery bag. I uncrumple it, hold it near my nose, and smell.

"Chocolate Danish."

I hold the open bag over my hand and some chocolate crumbs fall out.

"You can't eat that," Benny tells me. "Those crumbs have germs."

"No, they don't. The bakery lady wears

plastic gloves when she takes the Danish from the display and puts it in the bag. The crumbs fell off without anyone touching them."

That's what I say, but I don't eat the crumbs and I don't drop them onto the street. That would be littering. I drop them back in the bag.

We come to my building.

Benny says, "Those wrappers and that bag could not have come from someone on one of the higher floors. If they did, they wouldn't have landed so close to the building. They must have come from someone just on the other side of that corner window."

"Someone who really likes chocolate," I say.

Benny walks toward his house, and I walk into my building and into my apartment. I go to the kitchen and throw out the candy wrappers and the bakery bag.

"Did you eat all that?" Grandma asks.

I tell her about the Take Care of Our Neighborhood thing.

"So you didn't eat all that. You must be hungry."

"I am."

"Sit by the table and close your eyes."

Grandma puts a cracker sandwich in my hand. I taste it.

"Guava."

Grandma laughs and says I'm right.

I know jelly.

Chapter 3

I'M A LITTLE SCARED

IT'S TUESDAY MORNING. Benny is waiting for me by the front of my building.

He's never late.

He never forgets his homework.

He never has a wrong answer on a test.

I'll bet if on a math test the question is, "How much is 2 + 2?" and Benny answered

"367," our teacher would think, *Maybe he's right. He's always right. I need to check my work.*

I leave my building and stop. I check my backpack to be sure I have my homework. I'm not perfect like Benny is.

I have it.

"Look at this," Benny says. He shows me an empty plastic shopping bag, the kind you get when you buy groceries. "It's for litter, so you won't have to put candy wrappers in your pocket."

He thinks of everything.

At the next corner we find a coffee cup lid. Sometimes those things fly off like a small Frisbee. Benny puts it into the bag.

We walk slowly past yesterday's red brick apartment building, the one with the candy wrappers and bakery bag, but we don't find any litter. The curtain of the corner window is open a bit. I think I see someone looking out.

"Did you see him?" I ask.

"I saw a hand holding back the curtain and someone looking out, but I'm not sure if it was a man or a woman."

"Or a boy or a girl, someone our age," I say, "or a firefighter with a bad cough, or a lost bus driver, or a dolphin with flippers that look like hands, or even a four-headed purple-skinned alien."

"Take it easy," Benny tells me. "Give your imagination a rest. My parents know people in this building, the Silvers, the Liebers, and the Rosens, and none of them is an alien."

We stop at the corner near school and wait for the light to change and for the crossing guard to tell us to cross.

Benny says, "You may be right about

it being someone young. It was a small hand."

We walk into school and in the front hall is a big "Take Care of Our Neighborhood" sign. Near it is a huge trash can and beside the can is a stepladder. The trash can is bigger than me. I think it's even bigger than Rabbi Goodman. Benny gets on the stepladder and drops the coffee cup lid in the can.

After lunch Rabbi Goodman comes into our room. He's holding a clipboard with some paper attached. He quietly walks around, opens our coat closet and looks in, and writes on the paper.

"Very good," he says before he leaves. "Your room is nice and clean and that's important. The Talmud tells us to beware of what is not clean."

All during class I think about the "Take

Care of Our Neighborhood" program and about the hand in the window. I'm so busy thinking about litter and the mysterious hand that I hardly sneak-eat any jelly beans.

"Do you think there'll be throw-away stuff by that building?" I ask Benny as we leave school. "Do you think whoever is on the other side of the window will be watching us?"

"I don't know," Benny answers, "but if there are candy wrappers we'll put them in this bag."

About a block from school we find an apple core. Benny picks it up by the stem, like it's contaminated. He drops it in the bag.

As we get near the red brick apartment building, we walk slower. There's some-thing in the bushes by the corner window.

It looks like another candy wrapper. I look at the window. The curtain is held slightly open.

We walk very slowly across the grass toward the building.

"I don't like being watched," I tell Benny. "I'm a little scared."

"There's nothing to be scared of," Benny says, but he's also walking real slowly. He's scared, too.

I reach into the bushes for the wrapper, but it's not a wrapper. Well, it is but it's not. It's a wrapper of an unopened chocolate bar, the kind Mom sometimes buys for me at the kosher market.

I look up. The curtain is no longer being held open.

As we walk away from the building I tell Benny, "This is our lucky day, candy to share."

"It's not ours. We can't eat it. We have to return it."

"Return it! Who are we going to return it to?"

As I say that I feel something on the back, a paper. I turn the bar over and see this note: *I hope you like chocolate.*

Benny and I look at each other.

"It's ours," I say and rip off the wrapper. We share the chocolate and we do like it. We like it a lot.

Chapter 4

EAT YOUR CANDY

IT'S WEDNESDAY MORNING and you know where Benny is. He's waiting to walk with me to school.

He shows me a paper. On it he wrote, *Thanks for the candy, Benny.*

He says, "I left room for you to add your name."

He wants to give me his pen to sign the paper. I don't take it.

"We don't even know his name, so why are we thanking him?"

As we walk toward school, Benny shakes his head and asks, "If your grandmother gets on a bus and someone gives her his seat, what does she do?"

"She sits."

"What does she do next?"

"She opens the book she brought along and reads. Grandma loves to read."

"Aren't you forgetting something?"

I think for a moment.

"Is it an aisle seat or a window seat? If it's by the window, she might look out."

Benny stops walking. He's waiting for me to say something.

"Okay! Okay! She doesn't know the name of whoever gave her the seat, but she would say 'thank you.' "

I take Benny's pen and sign the note and add this: *What's your name?*

We get to the red brick apartment building and walk across the grass to the corner window. The curtain is closed. With one hand Benny holds the note against the glass so the message is facing in. With his other hand he takes a small tape dispenser from his pocket and sticks the note to the window.

A tape dispenser!

Benny thinks of everything.

After lunch Rabbi Goodman comes into our room again. He quietly walks around and then says, "Very good."

"We have two 'very goods,' " I tell Benny on our way home. "Maybe we'll win the party."

We're waiting at the corner near school.

The traffic light is red.

"I thought you didn't want the pizza."

I laugh.

"You're thinking like a Benny. Try thinking like an Eli. If we win, the party will be at the end of the day, when Mr. Moscowitz teaches us history, and I'm tired of learning about the American Revolution. For me the prize for winning isn't a pizza party on Monday. It's no history on Monday."

The light is green now. The guard lets us cross the street.

Did you know when the Revolution started Paul Revere wasn't the only one who rode from Boston calling out "The British are coming!"? William Dawes did that, too.

I ask Benny, "Do you know why everyone remembers Paul Revere and few people know about William Dawes? It's because of that poem by Henry Something Longfellow, 'The Midnight Ride of Paul Revere.'"

"Wadsworth," Benny tells me, "Henry Wadsworth Longfellow."

"Lots of stuff rhymes with Revere. Not like Dawes. Nothing rhymes with that."

"How about jigsaws, rickshaws, hee-haws, and Arkansas?" Benny asks. "Those rhyme with Dawes."

"Whatever. I'm just tired of hearing about the Revolution."

We're by the red brick apartment building. The curtains inside the corner window are closed, but there's a paper taped to the other side of the glass and something is written on it. Benny and I walk close enough to read it.

Hi. I'm Mendy Rosen. I hope you like

raisins.

Benny says, "He must be the son of the Rosens my parents know, the ones who live in this building."

On the ledge beneath the window are two wrapped chocolate bars, milk chocolate with raisins. I take one, open it, and start eating. It's really good.

Benny taps lightly on the window. When no one answers, he taps again, but not so lightly. Still, no one answers.

"Eat your candy," I tell Benny. "We can thank him tomorrow."

Chapter 5

BUZZ 1E

IT'S ODD.

Benny and I have a friend we've never seen. We know his name and I guess he's about our age. I guess that, but I don't really know. I'm happy Mendy gives us chocolate bars with raisins, but I'm sure that's not good enough for Benny. I don't know what he'll want, but I do know he'll want to do more than just thank him.

I like Benny, but sometimes he makes things too complicated.

"Hey," Benny calls to me as I come out of our building.

He's holding a paper. It's a message for Mendy. *Thanks again for the candy. My mother is Miriam Feder and she knows your family. How about we visit with you after school?* He signed it "Benny Feder" and left room for me to add my name.

I decide if Mendy and I are going to be friends he should know my nickname, so I sign the paper, "Jelly Eli Z."

We get to Mendy's building. The curtain by his window is closed. With one hand Benny holds the note against the glass with the message facing in.

With his other hand, he tapes the note to the window.

Benny lightly taps on the window.

We wait.

Benny taps again, louder this time.

Still no answer.

"Let's go," Benny says. "We can't be late for school."

We pick up some litter along the way and put it into Benny's bag. When we get to school I climb the stepladder and empty the bag into the huge trash can.

During lunch, Rabbi Goodman walks through the cafeteria. He stops by a few of the messier tables and tells the kids there, "When you're done, make sure you clean up."

Before we go back to class, Rabbi Goodman tells everyone that he will announce the pizza party winning class

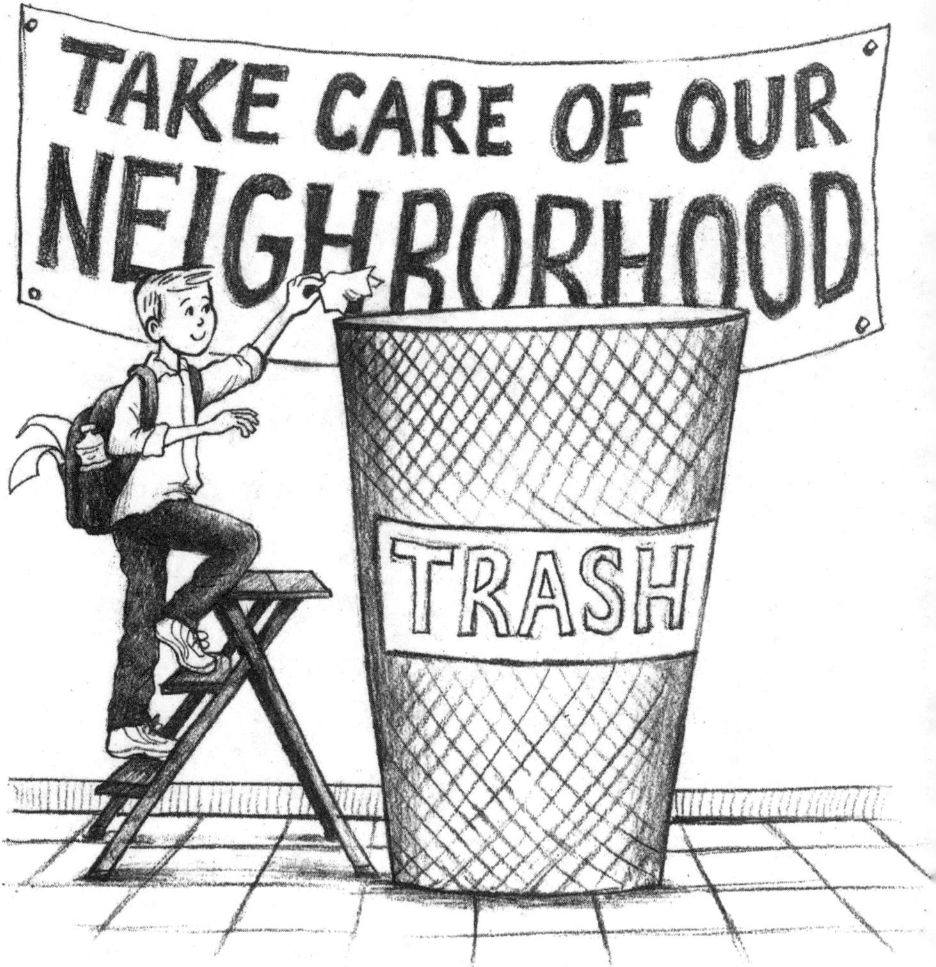
TAKE CARE OF OUR NEIGHBORHOOD
TRASH

at lunch on Monday.

We get back to class, and our room smells like a public bathroom. Our teacher, Mr. Moscowitz, is putting away a roll of paper towels and a spray container. I lean over my desktop and inhale. Ammonia. Mr. Moscowitz must have washed all the desks. And the floor looks freshly cleaned.

He must want our class to be judged the best at keeping our neighborhood clean. Maybe he really likes pizza.

Rabbi Goodman comes into our room. He quietly walks around. "Very good," he says before he leaves. "Your room is nice and clean. It even smells clean."

Ammonia.

That's our third "very good."

I don't know what Benny is thinking on our way home from school, but

I know what I'm thinking. I'm thinking chocolate.

We get near the red brick apartment building and I ask, "Do you think Mendy will be by the window?"

Benny hunches up his shoulders. That means he doesn't know.

We get closer and I see the curtain is open. The window is also open and someone is sitting there.

Mendy.

We walk across the grass to meet him.

He looks a little younger than us. Benny and I are ten. Maybe he's nine. He has dark hair and it's cut funny, like he cut it himself. And it looks like he's wearing a robe, the kind you wear when you're sick and it's over your pajamas. He's in a wheelchair.

"Which one of you is Benny and who's

Eli?" he asks.

We tell him.

"Do you want to visit?"

Benny and I look at each other. Benny's parents know the Rosens.

"Sure," we say. "We'll visit."

"Buzz 1E. My mom will let you in."

Chapter 6

HOMESCHOOLED

BENNY AND I GO to the entrance. The front door is not locked but the inside door is. Along the side wall is a panel of buttons. The name next to 1E is *Rosen*. I press it.

"Who's there?" a woman asks.

These security systems are spooky. We don't see anyone, but we hear her.

"Benny and Eli," I answer.

Bzzzzzz.

Benny opens the inside door and we walk in. A woman in a long dark skirt and a white shirt is standing by the open door to apartment 1E.

"Mendy is excited," she tells us. "He doesn't get many visitors."

As we follow her to Mendy's room I wonder, *Why does this woman look like someone I know?*

"Mendy," his mom says when we come to his room, "your friends are here."

He's sitting in a wheelchair beside his bed.

"Hi!" he says.

He waves to us so I know his hands and arms are okay. It's his legs. They're in braces.

There are two metal folding chairs so

we sit. There's a small table nearby. On it are some books.

"Look at my hair," he says. "It's a mess."

It is. One side is shorter than the other and the back is all choppy, like a beaver ate pieces of it. I know, beavers chew wood, but that's how his hair looks, chewed up.

"It's hard for Mom to take me out to a barber. She says it's easier to cut it herself. Usually, she does it better."

The window is by his bed. I recognize the curtains. Now I'm seeing them from the other side.

We talk for a while. He asks lots of questions about school because he's never been in one. He's being "home schooled". His mother is his teacher. The room we're in right now, his bedroom, is his classroom.

His mom comes in and asks, "Would you like something to drink, soda or milk? Would you like a snack?"

Before I can say yes, Benny says, "No, thank you."

I bet the snack would have been chocolate.

Mendy tells us, "This morning, I heard you knocking on the window, but my therapist was here and I was doing stretching exercises for my legs. Every morning after my exercises Mom gives me my school assignments and she goes off to work. She rewards me if I do them well."

"Does she reward you with candy?" I ask.

Mendy smiles.

"Yes, a bar of chocolate. Mom gets them from work."

"Work?"

"She helps at Rubin's. It's a small grocery store. Rubin is my uncle."

That's where I've seen her, when I shop with Grandma and my sister, Debbie. The candy he gave us must have been his reward for doing his schoolwork, his home-school work.

His mother comes in carrying a tray with a plate of chocolate squares and three glasses of milk. She puts it on the table beside the books.

"I know you said you didn't want anything. This is just in case you change your minds."

"Thank you," I say really quickly, before Benny has a chance to tell her we still don't want anything.

On the plate are squares of regular milk chocolate and white chocolate. I take a square of the regular and a sip of milk.

"We can't stay much longer," Benny says. "We have homework to do."

I quickly take two more squares.

Mrs. Rosen says, "You can do your homework here."

Benny tells her that the table really isn't big enough for all three of us to work on, and that we must get home.

"Before you go," she says, "could I see the homework? I'd like to see what you're studying."

Benny takes out our math and history homework sheets. They're not cut or copied from a workbook. Mr. Moscowitz makes them.

"These are really good," Mrs. Rosen says. "We're studying the same things. We follow the regular fourth grade curriculum."

Benny says he'll ask Mr. Moscowitz if he has extras. He says we'll be back again tomorrow.

Benny says all that without asking me. But that's okay. I want to visit again.

Chapter 7

MAGIC?

IT'S FRIDAY, the last day of the "Take Care
of Our Neighborhood–Pizza Party" thing.
Benny has his plastic shopping bag, and
on our way to school we find some things
to put in the bag. When we get to school
I climb the stepladder and empty the bag
into the trash can.

During lunch, Rabbi Goodman walks through the cafeteria with his clipboard and papers. He keeps stopping and writing.

A third grader stands several feet from the trash can, crumples his empty lunch bag into a ball, and throws it toward the can. "Basket! Two points," the boy calls as it flies from his hand.

But the balled-up bag doesn't land with the trash. It hits the lip of the can and bounces off as the boy turns and walks toward his table.

Rabbi Goodman writes something and then calls to the boy.

"David, come back here and pick that up."

"Oops!" David says.

He picks up the ball of paper and drops it into the trash can.

After lunch Rabbi Goodman comes into our room. He quietly walks around and writes on the paper. "Very good," he says before he leaves.

That's our fourth "very good."

That's very, very, very, very good!

I can almost taste the pizza and the warm orange soda.

"Don't rush out," Benny tells me when it's time to go home. "I want to talk to Mr. Moscowitz."

We wait for all the other kids to leave the room. I stand nearby as Benny tells Mr. Moscowitz about Mendy. He asks if he has any extra homework sheets.

"Yes, of course."

He takes a big box of papers from his closet. He gives Benny about twenty math, history, and science homework sheets. Maybe more.

On our way out of school Benny says, "Mendy will be so excited with all these sheets."

"We'll see," I say. I wonder why anyone would be happy to get all that homework.

In the front vestibule of Mendy's building, I press the button marked *1E*.

"Who's there?"

"Benny and Eli."

Bzzzzzz.

Mrs. Rosen is waiting for us. Three glasses of milk and lots of chocolate squares are on the small table in Mendy's room. Benny gives Mrs. Rosen the homework sheets. She looks at each one.

"These are terrific."

She's really happy.

Mendy doesn't look so happy.

"We don't get this much at once," I tell

him. "We get maybe two a day."

I ask Mendy what he does all day and he tells us.

"I do the schoolwork Mom gives me and I read a lot. I read biographies, chess books, and magic books."

"Magic?"

He takes a wooden cup from the drawer of his nightstand. He lifts the top of the cup and there's a small red ball.

"Take the ball and put it in my pocket."

I put the ball in his pajama pocket.

He puts the top back on the cup and asks, "Where's the ball?"

I point to his pocket.

"No, it's not there."

He lifts the top of the cup and there's the ball, just where it was before. He puts the top on the cup and asks again, "Where's the ball?"

I point to the cup.

"No," he says and lifts the top of the cup. It's not there. He takes the ball from his pocket and puts it in the cup.

"How did you do that?" Benny and I ask.

"A magician never reveals his secrets," he says and smiles. "But maybe I will, the next time you visit. And maybe next time we can play a game of chess."

"I know how to move the pieces," I say, "but I don't play that well."

Benny says, "I'm also not a good chess player."

"The two of you can team up against me."

Benny and I look at each other.

"Yes, we'll play," I say, "next time."

Chapter 8

BENNY AND ME

IT'S MONDAY. The pizza party contest is over but still, Benny has the shopping bag. On the way to school we pick up litter, an empty torn envelope, and a sneaker.

Now please tell me how someone could lose a sneaker. Does it fall off and he says, "Oh well, I'll hop."

Benny picks up the sneaker by the lace, like the sneaker is contaminated. He drops it into the bag. We get to school and the huge trash can is still there. Benny gets on the step ladder and drops the stuff we picked up into the can.

All morning I think about lunch, not eating it, but Rabbi Goodman's announcement. I want to know who won the party.

Now it's lunchtime. Rabbi Goodman is in the cafeteria. He walks from table to table and tells kids to throw junk away. Even though the contest is over, I guess he still wants the place to be clean.

Rabbi Goodman taps on the microphone. He wants us to be quiet.

"Today is the day," he says. "Last week you kept your classrooms, our playground, and the neighborhood

clean. You all cooperated. I chose the one class that I felt did the best job of it. Every time I checked, its room was clean. Its lunch tables were clean."

That could be us.

"What impressed me most was that every morning students from this class, especially two boys, threw litter they found outside in the big trash can I set in the hall."

I think the two boys he's talking about are Benny and me.

"Class 4M, I hope you like pizza!"

That's us! The kids at our two tables cheer.

That's it for the American Revolution. We won't learn about it today.

Hey, Paul Revere, here's something to shout. "Pizza and soda are coming! Pizza and soda are coming!"

It's time to return to class. Benny tells me to go without him. He wants to talk to Rabbi Goodman.

Why?

I sit in class and wait for Benny. He walks in and doesn't even look at me.

What's he up to with Rabbi Goodman?

Mr. Moscowitz teaches us some math.

Now there's a little more than a half hour left to class and I smell it, pizza.

Rabbi Goodman walks into our room pushing a cafeteria wagon. On the top shelf are four large pizza boxes. On the bottom shelf are paper plates and cups and bottles of soda, cola, ginger ale, and orange.

Yes, orange!

"Before I give out the pizza, you have a choice to make."

I think he's going to say, "You can have

regular pizza or Sicilian," but he doesn't.

He says, "You may stay here and celebrate with Mr. Moscowitz, or if you live close to Hamilton Street you may come with Benny, Eli, and me to a boy named Mendy Rosen's apartment."

Rabbi Goodman tells the class about Mendy. He knows Mrs. Rosen and he knows Mendy. Benny must have asked Rabbi Goodman if we could have the party there.

Six boys join us. Mrs. Rosen is waiting by the front door of the building. We follow her to apartment 1E. Mendy is in the dining room. Instead of pajamas, he's wearing regular clothes. There's a nice cloth on the table and plates of chocolate squares.

It's quite a party. We all have a good time, especially Mendy. Benny and I are the last to leave. Before we go, Mendy tells us, "Now I have two best friends and lots more."

I know who his best friends are.

Benny and me.

A Baseball Problem for
JELLY ELi Z.

Illustrated by Dena Ackerman

A Baseball Problem for
JELLY ELi Z.

From the author of the Cam Jansen series

DAVID A. ADLER

MENUCHA CLASSROOM SOLUTIONS

CONTENTS

Chapter 1

NiBBLE, NiBBLE BOYSENBERRY

"ICE CREAM."

It's Friday afternoon. We're in the middle of lots of kids leaving school and that's what my best friend, Benny, says. "Ice cream."

"Regular or soft serve?" I ask.

He looks at me like that's a strange question.

"You know," I tell him, "not all ice cream is the same. Soft serve is creamy and smooth because almost half of it is air. So are we talking about regular or soft serve, and why are we talking about ice cream?"

We stop at the corner and wait for the traffic light to change.

"It's because of Sunday. There's a choose-up baseball game at Brandeis Park and they need two more kids. Mendy Rosen told me about it. Sometimes his mom takes him to watch the game."

"Who plays?"

"It's mostly older boys and everyone on the winning team gets two scoops of ice cream, *regular ice cream*, from Mr. Perl."

The light changes to green and we cross

the street.

"What flavor?"

"Why do you ask so many questions?"

"Aha!" I say. "Now you asked a question."

Benny tells me I can be annoying. He's not the first person to say that.

He doesn't know the answers to all my questions about the Sunday game. This will be his first time playing at Brandeis Park.

I tell Benny, "There should be jelly-flavored ice cream."

He stops, turns, and looks right at me.

"The most popular flavor is vanilla and I don't understand that. No one asks for a peanut butter and vanilla sandwich. They want peanut butter and jelly."

"You would love jelly-flavored ice cream, wouldn't you, Jelly Eli Z.?"

I tell Benny, "This would be the great

thing about jelly-flavored ice cream. One scoop could be strawberry-flavored jelly and the next boysenberry. But with vanilla it's always the same. Vanilla."

"You and your jelly," Benny says and shakes his head.

We continue walking.

Most of the kids in our school live close enough to walk home. As we walk, boys go off in different directions until there are just the two of us, Benny and me.

"About the game," Benny says. "There's this old man named Mr. Perl and he lives with his son's family. Mrs. Rosen knows him and the old Mr. Perl's son is a friend of my dad's."

"So what you're saying is an old man has a son and your dad has a son of course, that's you. And the old man's son and your dad are friends."

"Exactly."

Benny is smart, but nothing is simple when he explains it.

"Old Mr. Perl has to sit in a wheelchair. Most Sunday mornings his son takes him to the park and once some boys were playing baseball. Old Mr. Perl had a great time watching the game, so now every Sunday his son makes sure there's one to watch. Kids call it, 'Old Mr. Perl's Sunday Game.' Two of the regulars can't play this week and Young Mr. Perl asked my dad if I could play and if I could bring a friend."

"I don't have a bat or a ball or a glove."

"They have extras."

"Okay," I say. "I'll play."

I'll go to Benny's house Sunday morning and we'll walk together to Brandeis Park.

My grandmother is waiting for me when I get home with a snack of jelly on crackers and a glass of milk. I sit by the kitchen table. I close my eyes. Grandma puts a cracker sandwich in my hand. I taste it.

"Boysenberry."

Grandma laughs and says, "You're right. Now finish eating and help me set the table for dinner."

On Friday night mom and Grandma light Shabbat candles and we eat together in the dining room. I nibble until every last bit of the boysenberry sandwich is gone. Then I take four dinner plates from the kitchen cabinet, one for Grandma, one for Mom, one for my sister Debbie and one for me and set them on the dining room table.

Chapter 2

TWEET! TWEET!

IT'S SUNDAY.

"*Bam!*" I say really loud and swing my pretend bat. "*Bam!*"

"Be careful with that," Benny says.

"With what?"

"With the bat."

I look at my hands. I'm not holding

anything.

"Okay," I tell Benny. "I won't swing my imaginary bat near any imaginary people."

Benny and I walk into the park. There are swings, seesaws, and lots of benches. We go to a flat grassy area. Four bases are laid out, making a narrow baseball field, not big enough for a full team of nine players but big enough for a game.

A bunch of boys are playing catch. They all look older than us.

On the side of the field, close to what must be home plate, are two men. One is in a wheelchair. One isn't. Benny calls one "Old Mr. Perl" and one "Young Mr. Perl," but they both look old to me. We walk over to meet them.

"Hi, Benny," the young Mr. Perl, who is not so young, says. "Thanks for coming and for bringing your friend."

"His name is Eli."

"Hi, Eli."

We shake hands and he says, "I'm Danny Perl and this is my father, Mr. Perl."

The man in the wheelchair smiles and asks, "Do you know why people call me Mr. Perl?"

I shake my head. How would I know that?

"It's because that's my name."

"That makes sense," I tell him, and it does.

"When I was your age I played baseball. Lots of it. I was a shortstop. Everyone wanted me on their team. I could also hit a few."

"A few?"

"You know. I could hit a ball a few hundred feet, real far. I hit singles and doubles. I didn't hit many triples and home runs because I wasn't real fast. I never had good legs. It's my legs that told me to stop. That's why I'm in a wheelchair. It's my legs."

Sometimes I swing a pretend baseball bat and he pretends, too. Right now he's pretending his legs talk to him, that they told him to stop playing baseball. Everyone pretends.

Young Mr. Perl asks, "How are you, Benny? How are all your siblings?" He turns and tells his father, "He has seven brothers and sisters."

"They're all fine."

"Let's get started," Old Mr. Perl tells his son. "We have twelve players."

I didn't notice it before, but Old Mr. Perl has a chain around his neck with a whistle hanging from it.

Tweet! Tweet!

He blows the whistle and waves for

everyone to come in. They gather around the wheelchair and some of them are a lot bigger than Benny and me.

"These two boys are Benny and Eli," Old Mr. Perl says. "They're new here so I'm going to tell you all things most of you know, but they don't."

"I'm the designated catcher," his son says, "and I'll divide you into teams."

"And I'm the umpire," his father tells us. "Each team will have a pitcher, three infielders, and two outfielders. We play six innings."

I know this stuff.

He looks at us to be sure we're all listening and says a bit louder, "Batters get two swings but don't think you can stand there and let every pitch go by. If you let three good ones go I'll call you out."

He waits and then asks, "Is that

understood? You get two swings and no more than three good pitches."

Everyone says he understands.

His son says, "Tell them about the ice cream."

"Yes. After the game every player gets ice cream. Those on the winning team get two scoops each. The others get one scoop."

Tweet! Tweet!

Mr. Perl blows his whistle and says, "Let's get started."

Chapter 3

THAT SECOND SCOOP

YOUNG MR. PERL divides us into two teams.

"You don't know the other boys," he tells Benny and me, "so I'm putting you together."

"And I'm Josh," a boy on our team tells us. "I'm the captain."

Josh is big, real big.

I whisper to Benny, "I'll bet he's in high school."

"I heard that! I'm in sixth grade. I just have big bones."

The other players on our team gather around Josh.

Josh says, "We bat first."

One at a time he points at the three other boys and tells them, "First, second, third, and I'll bat fourth. That's the cleanup spot. It's called that because after one or all of you get on base, *bam!* I'll clean it all up. I'll hit a long ball, a home run."

He turns and looks at Benny and me.

"You'll bat after me," he tells Benny. "And Little One, you'll bat last."

He called me "Little One"!

I'm not really little for my age. But he's older. He's two grades ahead of me.

There are two benches on the sideline close to first base. Benny and I sit on one of them. The rest of our team sits on the other.

"Don't think of yourself as batting last," Benny tells me. "You're batting sixth."

"Sixth is last. And I'm not 'Little One.' I'm Eli."

The other team is on the field.

In the middle of the infield is their pitcher. I think I've seen him in school and he's in fifth grade, but I'm not sure. He's not much bigger than Benny and me.

There's a boy standing near first base and another near third and there's a boy in the middle of the infield. The boy near first is about as big as Josh.

There are two boys in the outfield.

Young Mr. Perl is behind home plate. He's the catcher.

Josh talks to each of the other players on our team. Then he comes to us.

"You boys are new here so you should know, we all do our best. We play hard."

He starts to walk away. Then he turns. "We need to win," he says. "I need that second scoop."

Chapter 4

LET'S PLAY BALL!

TWEET! TWEET!

"Let's play ball!" Old Mr. Perl shouts in his gruff voice.

"Let's go, Izzy," Josh tells our first batter. "Hit it a mile."

Izzy stands by home plate. He's in sixth grade, but he's about my size. He holds his bat back and waits for the pitch.

Here it comes.

It's right over the plate, a great pitch. Izzy doesn't swing.

"That was a good one," Old Mr. Perl says. "That's one strike. Two more and I'll call you out."

Izzy doesn't swing at the second pitch.

Mr. Perl tells him, "That was also good."

Josh is walking back and forth along the side of the field. "Let's go," he says. "Hit one."

The next pitch is high. This time Izzy swings and misses.

"One out," Old Mr. Perl says.

Izzy gives the bat to Jacob, the second batter, who stands at the other side of home plate. He's a lefty.

The first pitch bounces just before it gets to home plate. Jacob doesn't swing.

"Good eye! Good eye!" Josh says.

He's still walking back and forth along the side of the field.

The next pitch is a good one. Jacob swings and hits it hard on the ground along the right side of the field. It scoots past the big kid playing first base.

Jacob carefully puts the bat on the ground. Then he runs to first.

"No, no, no," Josh says and shakes his head. "Drop the bat. Drop the bat and run."

Aaron is the third batter. He hits an easy-to-catch ball to the pitcher.

There are two outs and it's Josh's turn to hit.

He stands by home plate. He taps his bat on the ground, looks toward the pitcher, and waits.

The two players in the outfield take several steps back. They're a long way out. I could never hit a ball that far.

The pitcher looks in at Josh. He looks nervous. I'll bet he's afraid to pitch to him. But he does. He throws the ball. It comes in right over the plate. Josh just watches it go by and into Young Mr. Perl's glove.

"That was a good one," Old Mr. Perl says.

"Yes, it was," Josh says. "It just wasn't good enough."

The next pitch is good, too, but Josh doesn't swing.

"One more," Old Mr. Perl tells him, "and you'll be out."

The next pitch is right over the center of home plate. Josh swings. He hits the ball high and far into the outfield. He drops the bat and runs toward first base.

One of the outfielders stands just where he was and waits.

Josh reaches first base and keeps

running. Jacob runs past second and is on his way to third base.

Old Mr. Perl moves in his wheelchair so he can see if the outfielder catches the ball. He does.

Tweet! Tweet!

Old Mr. Perl blows his whistle and shouts, "Three outs!"

"Did you see that? Did you see how far I hit the ball?" Josh asks as he runs off the field. "*Pow!* It was almost a home run."

But it wasn't, I think. *It was just another out.*

Josh tells each of us what position we'll play. "Little One," he tells me, "you'll be in the outfield with me."

Benny and I borrow gloves from players on the other team.

Benny walks onto the field with me and whispers, "Josh really hit that ball."

"An out is an out," I whisper back.

I walk to the outfield and Josh points to where he wants me to stand. He wants me all the way to the right, where it's not likely any balls will be hit. He's in the middle of the outfield. I'm sure he expects to get just about every ball that's hit out here.

Tweet! Tweet!

Old Mr. Perl blows his whistle.

"Batter up!" he shouts. "Batter up!"

Chapter 5

LET'S GO, JELLY ELI!

THE OTHER TEAM'S batter *is* up. He's standing by home plate ready to hit. I'm ready, too, ready to catch the ball if it comes out here, but it probably won't. Benny is standing near second base. He's also ready.

Jacob is our pitcher. He looks in at Young Mr. Perl. He swings his arm around as if he's pitching in the big leagues.

He's pretending.

Here's the pitch. The batter swings and hits the ball hard on the ground to Benny's left. Benny is quick. He gets the ball and throws it to our first baseman.

Old Mr. Perl turns his wheelchair and rolls it closer to first base so he can watch the play.

"One out!"

Mr. Perl rolls his wheelchair back, closer to home plate.

The next batter stands with the bat on his shoulder. Here's the first pitch. He swings late.

"That's one swing," Old Mr. Perl tells him. "One more and you're out."

In big league baseball, a batter gets three swings. And if he hits foul balls he gets even more. But this isn't big league baseball. It's not even Little League. It's Old Mr. Perl's Sunday game.

Here's the second pitch. The batter swings late again.

"Two swings. You're out."

It's the other team's first baseman's turn to hit. He's big.

"Hit one, Big Sol!" one of his teammates shouts.

I take several steps back.

The first pitch is low. Sol watches it go by.

The second pitch comes in right over home plate. Big Sol swings.

Thwack!

Oh no!

The ball is high and headed to the outfield, and not toward Josh. It's coming to me.

I take a few more steps back and wait.

I can do this.

Here it comes.

The ball is about to land in my glove when Josh runs in front of me. He catches the ball.

Tweet! Tweet!

"Three outs!" Old Mr. Perl shouts.

"Pretty great!" Josh says. "It's a good thing I caught that."

"No, it's not a good thing," I tell him as we walk in from the outfield. "That was my ball. I'm on this team, too."

"Sure, sure. You're on this team, too."

The way he says that I don't think he really believes it. Everyone knows that baseball is a team game. Everyone but Josh.

Benny is waiting for me by our bench when I come off the field. He's holding the bat. "I'm up and then it's your turn."

Benny wears glasses. He looks like a scholar. And he is. But he's also good at sports.

He stands by home plate. He holds his bat back and waits.

Here it comes. The pitch is low. Benny doesn't swing.

Benny swings at the next pitch and hits the ball really hard. It zooms just about two feet above the grass. It's just out of Sol's reach.

Benny drops the bat and runs. By the time the boy playing in the outfield, about where I play, throws the ball in, Benny is standing on second base. He hit a double.

Now it's my turn.

"Take a few steps back," Sol tells his team. "These new guys can really hit."

Benny can. I can't.

Benny is standing on second base. The

score is tied. Zero to zero. It's up to me to hit the ball.

"Let's go, Little One!" Josh shouts. "Get a hit!"

Yeah, Jelly Eli, I tell myself. *Let's go.*

Chapter 6

RUN! RUN!

I STAND BY home plate and look out at
the field. The two players in the outfield
are way out, about where they were
when Josh was up. I could never hit a
ball that far. Even the players in the
infield are playing deep, like I'm some
great slugger. I'm not.

I tap the bat on the ground and look toward the pitcher, and wait. That's what Josh did and he hit the ball pretty far.

Here comes the first pitch.

It comes in fast and right over the plate. I watch it go by and into Young Mr. Perl's glove.

That's what Josh did.

"That was a good one," Old Mr. Perl says.

I hold my bat back and wait for the next one. The next pitch is good, too. This time I close my eyes and swing as hard as I can.

I hit the ball!

Well, I don't really hit the ball. I touch the ball with my bat and it rolls slowly toward third base. I drop the bat and run. Benny runs, too.

The boy playing third base runs in to get the ball. But he was playing much too deep. By the time he has it, I'm standing on first base.

I hardly hit the ball. If the boy playing third had been playing where he usually does, I would have been out.

"That's it! That's it!" Josh shouts and claps his hands. "That's smart baseball, Little One."

I wasn't smart. I was lucky. I was trying to hit the ball really hard, but all I hit was a dribbler. But here I am standing on first base and Benny is on third. One more hit and we'll score a run.

Our next batter is Izzy.

"Let's go," Josh yells. "Hit it a mile."

The other team doesn't think he'll hit it a mile. They move in.

Izzy stands by home plate. He holds his bat back and waits for the pitch.

Here it comes.

It's a good pitch, but Izzy doesn't swing.

"That's one strike," Old Mr. Perl says.

"Don't just stand there," Josh tells him.

The next two pitches come in really high, almost out of reach, and Izzy swings both times.

"One out," Old Mr. Perl says.

It's Jacob's turn.

He swings at the first pitch and misses. He swings and hits the next pitch hard on the ground along the right side of the field. He's about to carefully put the bat on the ground.

"Drop it! Drop the bat!" Josh shouts.

Jacob drops the bat and runs to first.

Sol hurries to his right and gets the ball. He runs with it to first base and gets there before Jacob does.

I run to second base. Benny runs home.

"Two outs," Mr. Perl says. "One run scores."

Yes! We're winning, 1–0.

The next batter is Aaron and he hits the ball hard on the ground to the left of the third baseman. It rolls into the outfield.

"Run! Run!" Josh and the others on my team yell.

Aaron runs. I run, too.

I step on third base and keep going. The ball is still rolling in the outfield when I reach home.

Yes! Now we're winning, 2–0.

Aaron is standing on second base.

Guess whose turn it is to hit.

Yes, you guessed it. Josh.

He stands by home plate and takes two mighty practice swings. He taps his bat on the ground, looks toward the pitcher, and waits.

The pitcher throws the ball. It comes in right over the plate and Josh swings. He took a mighty swing, but he missed.

I watch the ball go into Young Mr. Perl's glove.

"That's one swing," Old Mr. Perl says.

Josh swings at the next pitch, too, and misses.

"Two swings. You're out," Old Mr. Perl says.

"Yeah, I'm out," Josh says and shakes his head. "But did you see that swing! If I'd hit that ball we'd still be looking for it. *Pow!* It would have been a home run."

But he didn't hit the ball. Benny, Jacob, Aaron, and I did, and we're winning 2–0.

Chapter 7

WHOOSH! THWACK!

"GOOD HIT," Izzy tells me as we walk onto the field. "All I do is swing and miss."

"You'll hit one," I say. "And we're winning. That's what matters."

Izzy stops by third base. That's where he plays. Josh and I go to the outfield.

Young Mr. Perl walks onto the field.

He holds up his hands and calls, "Time!" Someone is being wheeled across the field. It's our friend Mendy. His mother pushes his wheelchair to the side of the field next to Old Mr. Perl.

Mendy waves to Benny and me and we wave back.

Through the next few innings there are a few hits, some errors, and a bunch of strikeouts. But there are no more runs. We're still winning 2-0. It's now the end of the sixth inning, the last inning. It's the other team's last chance to hit.

Jacob looks in at Young Mr. Perl. Jacob swings his arm around. He's still pretending that he's pitching in the big leagues. But he's not pitching as well as he was when the game started. I guess he's getting tired.

His first pitch is too high. His next pitch

is too low. His third pitch is just right.

Hey, this sounds like *Goldilocks and the Three Bears.*

Big Sol is the batter. He swings and hits the third pitch over Izzy's head and into the outfield. It bounces twice before Josh can get to it.

It's a double.

This inning doesn't begin well and it doesn't go well. The next batter gets a hit. Sol runs to third and then home. We're still winning, but now we're ahead by just one run. The score is 2–1.

There's a runner on first base.

The third hitter in the inning also gets a hit. Now there are two runners on base.

"Time-out!" Josh shouts.

Tweet! Tweet!

Old Mr. Perl blows his whistle. Mendy puts his hands over his ears. His mother moves him away. That whistle must sound pretty loud when you're right next to it.

Josh runs into the infield. He talks to Jacob. Most of the players on our team join them. Only Benny and I stay where we are.

I wave to Benny and he waves back.

Josh is probably saying something very clever to Jacob like, "Don't pitch too high. Don't pitch too low. Pitch just right and get him out!"

Tweet! Tweet!

"Let's go!" Old Mr. Perl shouts.

Josh runs back to the outfield.

Jacob does pitch just right. The next batter swings twice and misses. There's one out.

The batter after that hits the ball on the ground toward third base. Izzy has it.

"Step on third! Step on third!" Josh shouts.

Izzy steps on third. There are two outs.

"Now throw it! Throw to first!" Josh shouts.

Izzy throws to first, but he waited too long. The batter is safe.

There are runners on first and second base.

"One more!" Josh shouts. "One more out and we win."

We *must* get him out. The batter after him is Big Sol.

Jacob swings his arm around. Here it comes.

WHOOSH!

The batter takes a mighty swing. He's trying to hit the ball way out of the park, but he misses.

With a swing like that he could hit the ball over my head. I take a few steps back. One more swing and miss and we win the game, but a hit could lose it for us.

Young Mr. Perl throws the ball back to our pitcher.

Jacob looks in. He swings his arm around once. He swings his arm around again, a double windup! At last he throws the ball.

WHOOSH!

THWACK!

The batter hits the ball hard and it's coming to me. I take a few quick steps back.

No!

I went the wrong way. The ball is going to bounce in front of me.

I run forward. I stretch my glove out in front of me, close to the ground.

I feel it!

I feel it!

I feel the ball in my glove!

"We win! We win!" Josh shouts. "That's three outs. We win!"

Chapter 8

NEXT WEEK, PISTACHIO

I LOOK TOWARDS home plate. Old Mr. Perl has wheeled his chair along the side of the field. He's close to first base.

"Did you catch it?" he shouts to me.

I guess he couldn't see the play.

"Of course he did!" Josh says.

"Did you?" Mr. Perl asks again.

I shake my head.

"No," I tell him. "It bounced into my glove."

The runners who had been on first and second base have already reached home. They scored. Because I didn't catch the ball their team wins the game, 3–2.

Josh throws his glove down. He kicks it toward the infield.

"Who does that?" he shouts at me. "Who tells an umpire he didn't catch the ball!"

I don't answer him, but I think, *I do that. I tell the truth.*

Benny is waiting for me by second base. "You did the right thing," he says.

All the other boys have gone ahead. They are standing by Mr. Perl's wheelchair. We join them.

"I thought you caught it," Izzy whispers.

"No. It took a short hop. My glove was close to the grass and it took a little bounce before it landed in my glove."

Benny and I are next to Mendy.

"I saw that," Mendy whispers to me. "I saw the ball touch the grass before you got it. "

"Yes," his mother whispers. "Our Torah doesn't say 'Win the game.' It does say many times, 'Tell the truth.'"

Tweet! Tweet!

Old Mr. Perl blows his whistle and calls out, "Here comes the ice cream."

The front door of the house closest to first base opens. His son comes out. He's pushing a cart. On it are plastic bowls, spoons, and two containers of ice cream.

"Line up, first the winning team and then the others."

Izzy is last in line and I'm just ahead of him. In front of me is Benny.

Izzy tells us, "There are always two flavors, vanilla and something else."

This week the other flavor is strawberry.

Old Mr. Perl asks the first boy in line, "What would you like?"

He takes two scoops of vanilla.

Some boys want one scoop of each flavor. But most boys choose just vanilla.

The winning team not only gets two scoops, they also get to choose the flavor they want. By the time it's our turn there may be no more vanilla. That's okay. I prefer strawberry.

Old Mr. Perl gives Mendy two scoops.

"Maybe next week I'll have chocolate. I know that's your favorite."

Josh is the first from our team to get ice cream.

"I'll take one of each, one scoop of vanilla and one scoop of strawberry."

Old Mr. Perl looks at Josh and shakes his head. "No," he says. "Your team didn't win. You get one scoop."

"Vanilla."

Benny chooses strawberry. Now it's my turn.

Mr. Perl smiles and tells me, "For being honest, you get two scoops."

"No. My team lost. I get one scoop and I'd like strawberry."

I introduce Izzy and Jacob to Mendy. They sit with Benny and me on the grass next to Mendy's wheelchair and eat our ice cream.

Izzy tells us, "There's lots more homework in sixth grade."

"We get enough in fourth grade," I say. "Sometimes we get too much."

I think any homework is too much.

Young Mr. Perl is walking toward us. He no longer has the cart. I guess he brought the leftover ice cream back to his house. He tells Benny and me, "I hope you'll be here for our next Sunday game."

We both tell him we will.

"We lost," I say, "but it was fun."

He smiles and tells us, "Next week we'll have chocolate and pistachio."

"I'll have chocolate," Mendy says.

"I'll have pistachio," I say, "one scoop if we lose and two if we win."

AUTHOR'S NOTE

ELI'S BASEBALL DILEMMA, should he tell an umpire the truth, is not a new one. It famously happened to William "Dummy" Hoy.

Hoy was born in Ohio in 1862. A childhood illness left him deaf and because he couldn't hear words he didn't learn to speak them. As a youngster Hoy discovered baseball. He loved the game and when he was old enough he became a professional baseball player.

Nicknames have always been popular in sports. Years ago, people who could not hear and speak were wrongly called "deaf and dumb," so William was given the not very nice nickname "Dummy". He was not embarrassed by his disabilities.

He played on professional teams in Oshkosh, Buffalo, St. Louis, Cincinnati, Louisville, Chicago, and Los Angeles. "In a game I played for Oshkosh," he remembered years later, "a line drive was batted into my centerfield position... I ran in fast and made the catch on a short pick-up." His teammates and fans in the stand were sure he had caught the ball. But when the umpire asked in sign language if he had, Hoy shook his head – No.

Hoy played for fourteen years in the Major Leagues. He was a good hitter and an outstanding fielder.

On October 7, 1961 ninety-nine year old William Hoy threw out the ceremonial first pitch of the third game of the World Series. He was being honored as the oldest living former Major League ballplayer. But he was much more than that. He was an honest and good man.